The Switch on the Back of the Moon

"Take off please, Timothy," ordered Captain Peregrine.

"Take off, aye," replied Timothy, grabbing the red and green knobs and pushing them slowly forward as far as they would go.

At once there was a tremendous whooshing noise from the engines and powdery green smoke engulfed the van as it lifted off and melted the hopscotch patch.

If you enjoy this book, then you'll want to read
The Plug at the Bottom of the Sea – **another exciting
Timothy Thompson adventure!**

**And here are even *more* adventure stories
from Young Hippo!**

The Thing From Knucker Hole
Herbie Brennan

The Bubblegum Tree
Chocolate Money Mystery
Bursting Balloons Mystery
Alexander McCall Smith

The Secret in the Storm
Ruth Silvestre

BRICE AVERY

The Switch on the Back of the Moon

Illustrated by John Eastwood

For my mother,
a.k.a. Dubious Gladys

Scholastic Children's Books,
Commonwealth House, 1-19 New Oxford Street,
London WC1A 1NU, UK
a division of Scholastic Ltd
London ~ New York ~ Toronto ~ Sydney ~ Auckland

Published in the UK by Scholastic Ltd, 1998

Text copyright © Brice Avery, 1998
Illustrations copyright © John Eastwood, 1998

ISBN 0 590 11306 2

Printed by Cox & Wyman Ltd, Reading, Berks.

2 4 6 8 10 9 7 5 3 1

Chapter 1

"The world famous astronomer inches his way up the slippery path to his observatory, perched high on the mountain peak," grunted Timothy Thompson as he crawled up the mossy roof of his house towards the chimney-stack at one end. Tied on his back he had a folding metal deck-chair, the duvet off his bed, a small wicker picnic hamper, an oil lamp and a long fat browny-red tube. The picnic hamper had been a gift from his Aunt Tabitha and the tube was an antique copper map-barrel given to him by his Uncle Peregrine. Tabitha and Peregrine weren't his real uncle and aunt but they were the only grown-ups who had ever looked after him and not had to be taken away in an ambulance, driven very slowly so as to avoid the bumps.

Leaning against the chimney, Timothy sprung open the deck-chair and hung it on two rusty metal hooks that stuck out of the brickwork. Then, taking care not to slip, he swung himself up into the seat and wrapped his duvet around him.

"What I really need is my own space station," he announced to no one in particular. "Preferably one shaped like a doughnut with a little kitchen and a few bunk-beds and an observation dome for my telescope."

An owl landed on the opposite chimney and looked at him oddly, so he didn't say any more, but made a mental note to put a space station on his Christmas present list. Next he balanced the picnic hamper on a handy ledge, lit the oil lamp and looked at his watch.

"Midnight," he announced to the owl.

"Time to map the constellation of Orion so I can finally decode the Violetta Stone."

The Violetta Stone was a piece of black marble the size and shape of a cannon-ball. It had a polished surface with thousands of tiny dots carved in it, spiralling down in a long winding procession from the top to the bottom.

It had been in the school museum for as long as anyone could remember and Timothy was trying to translate it for his history project. Many famous archaeologists had examined it, and had declared the little patterns of dots to be unknown hieroglyphs. But Timothy, because he was a brilliant astronomer, had recognized the dots for what they were. He had discovered that the ancient Mesopotamians, whose stone it was, had made a secret code using the constellations of the night sky instead of an alphabet. It was a code that only someone who really loved the stars would understand.

"When the dots make the shape of the Plough you go 'daa'," he explained to the owl. "And when they look like Cassiopeia

you go 'ish'. So when they are together on the stone you say 'da-ish' which, as everyone knows, is ancient Mesopotamian for fire-ball."

The owl flew off to hunt for 'la-fon'* leaving Timothy to look for the constellation of Orion, the last shape he needed to begin deciphering the ancient code so carefully carved in the stone thousands of years ago.

(* Big-Mice in Mesopotamian)

The clouds parted and there above the trees that fringed the allotments hung Orion the Mighty Hunter, shining bright and strong – two shoulders, two feet, a head, a belt and a sword, all picked out in pinpoints of light. Timothy took the cap off one end of his copper map-barrel, slid out his telescope and charts and began to mark the stars with coloured pens. Despite the cold, he worked steadily, making dots on the paper until he'd drawn the whole outline.

"Of course, we can only see the brightest stars," he said to no one in particular. "The street lights make sure of that."

It wasn't just the street lights that were a problem. All the bulbs that burned in the towns and villages round about and in the factories and cities of the world all shone light into the sky as well. So anyone looking up from the earth could only see the very brightest few thousand stars. Timothy felt a bit sad about this and suddenly realized how cold his toes and feet had got.

"A nice beaker of hot Jungle Juice is what you need, Timbo my lad." He laughed out loud at his imitation of Aunt Tabitha, and reached into the hamper for his Thermos.

As he sipped the warming juice he looked up again at Orion and noticed something odd. Above Orion's belt a light had appeared where before there had been nothing at all.

"It looks like he's got a tummy button," chuckled Timothy as he focused his telescope.

Instead of a sharp point like a star or the flashing of a distant aeroplane he saw a fuzzy pinky-white blob. Timothy thought to himself for minute and then looked again, only to find that whatever it was had got a tiny bit bigger.

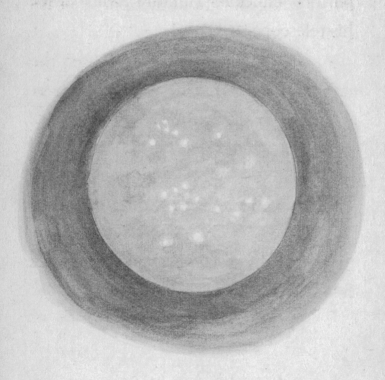

"The only thing that appears from nowhere, is fuzzy and gets bigger and brighter, is a comet," he mused excitedly, wondering if he was the first astronomer to see it. "But comets have tails and I can't see the tail on this one – so it's either going straight away from us or it's coming straight towards us."

At that moment Timothy realized the importance of what he'd seen. Without another look he gathered up his things, ran along the ridge of the roof and jumped in through his bedroom window. Pausing only to telephone the duty astronomer at the Royal Observatory and report his discovery, he went to wake his parents.

Chapter 2

Timothy's parents were both fast asleep because they had to be up early the next morning to go into their laboratory. They were famous scientists and were always busy with important experiments. Timothy rushed into their room and turned on the light.

"There's a comet coming out of

Orion's tummy button and it's getting bigger and it's got no tail which is impossible so it's straight out the back which means it's coming directly at us," he announced breathlessly.

"That's nice, dear," replied his mother, half asleep.

"Go to bed," mumbled his father crossly.

Timothy, who could see he was getting nowhere, went round to his father's side of the bed and hit him gently but firmly on the temple with his copper map-barrel. In an instant, Mr Thompson was sitting up in bed, wide awake and rubbing his head.

"What happened?" he said.

"I hit you on the head to get your attention because there's a comet just appeared in the constellation of Orion and it's going to hit the earth."

His father caught sight of the Thermos in Timothy's other hand.

"You've been drinking too much of that funny juice Uncle Peregrine left behind," he said. "I'll bet it's full of E-numbers."

"Don't be silly, dear," said his wife, sitting up. "I'm sure it's quite harmless. Timothy's just overtired."

Timothy was wondering what to do next when the telephone rang, which was an odd thing for it to do at one in the morning. Mr Thompson answered it and when he rang off he was very pale.

"That was the Secretary General of the United Nations. There's a comet coming straight for the earth," he said, getting up and going to the window.

"They want us to go to an emergency conference," he continued. "All the other scientists are going too."

"Oh dear, not another world-threatening disaster," sighed Timothy's mother, looking at the comet, which was now about the size of a peppercorn held at arm's length and getting bigger all the time. "You'll have to come with us again," she continued, turning to Timothy.

"Only this time you'd better keep out of trouble," added his father, remembering their last emergency conference at the United Nations when Timothy had appeared through a ventilation duct above the head of the Secretary General. He was in the middle of announcing that a brand-new and perfectly good space station was going to be abandoned and allowed to drift into outer space because no one could agree on what colour to paint it. Timothy had tried to ask if he could have it, because it had a little kitchen and some bunk-beds and an observation bubble that would just fit his telescope. Unfortunately, the ventilation grille dropped on the Secretary General's head and Timothy just got told off and made to sit in the car.

"Why don't you let me stay at home?" asked Timothy, knowing perfectly well what the reply would be.

"Because nobody can be found who will risk coming to look after you, so you'll have to come with us."

"What about Uncle Peregrine and Aunt Tabitha?" he suggested. "They looked after me last time and the police didn't come round once."

"But you ended up in Siberia and it cost a fortune to get you all back, not to mention the remains of the bathysphere," retorted his father. (You can read all about the bathysphere in another Timothy Thompson Adventure, *The Plug at the Bottom of the Sea*.) "Besides, I don't think they are fit to be left in charge. They always get overexcited and that's when the trouble

22

starts. Anyway, we don't have their phone number," he drivelled on, making up excuses as he went.

It was now very late, so Timothy's mother booked a taxi for eight in the morning and went back to bed.

Timothy, who was still dressed, had other plans. As soon as he heard his father stop grumbling about everything and start snoring, he pulled out a little leather pouch from a secret compartment and undid the drawstring.

Inside was a long piece of bright green cloth with a dried marsupial skull on the end. With practised steps that avoided all the tell-tale creaking floorboards, he crept downstairs, eased open the door of his house, crossed the frosty grass and hung the skull on the gate so that it swung invitingly in the breeze. In his mind he remembered Uncle Peregrine's words: "If you need us just hang out the skull and we'll come as soon as we can."

Back in his bedroom, Timothy sat at his desk and turned on the lamp. He had to prepare his talk for assembly in the morning. Spread out before him were his charts and notebooks, but in the centre was a large, black marble sphere. It was the Violetta Stone. Mr Boggins the headmaster had been very cross and made a fuss when he wanted to borrow it. Eventually Timothy was forced to apply pressure by reminding him how long it took to clean up the school after the mysterious plague of killer gerbils the previous term. Purple with rage, Boggins gave in, but not without an extended bout of muttering along the lines of: "Not used to being blackmailed in my own school" and "Pretty shrewd idea who was responsible for the plague".

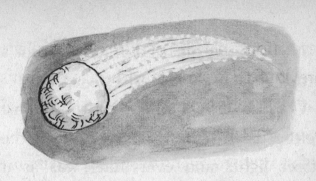

All through the night, while Timothy worked at decoding the hieroglyphs, the comet, which was as big as France but still only looked as if it was a burning lentil, thundered on through the silent ocean of space.

By first following the dots on the stone, then saying the words out loud and then looking them up in his Dictionary of Ancient Mesopotamian, Timothy cracked the code.

"Amazing and only just in time," he yawned, reading his notebook and looking forward to revealing his results to the school in the morning.

Next he put his head in his arms for a little rest and fell fast asleep.

Outside it was the darkest time – just before dawn. The dew glistened in the street lights and everything was as it should have been. Everything, that is, except the strange light in the sky from the comet, which had grown to the size of a red-hot Brussels sprout, and the noise of a large and very well-tuned engine.

The engine belonged to an enormous black removal van which now turned the corner of Timothy's road and trundled to a gentle gravel-crunching halt outside his house. On its roof was a giant grab on a telescopic arm. From inside the cab came the noise of two people laughing and joking and generally getting over-excited.

Before it was properly light, a noise woke Timothy from a dream in which he was being awarded the Nobel Prize for Extreme Cleverness.

Something or someone was tapping on the window with what sounded suspiciously like a pair of pickled onion tongs.

Jumping up from where he had been slumped over his notes and rubbing his eyes, Timothy pulled back the curtains and saw two smiling faces peering in.

It was Aunt Tabitha and Uncle Peregrine.

Aunt Tabitha waved the onion tongs and rattled her enormous earrings. Timothy pulled up the window.

"You've come," he gasped.

"Of course we have," she replied. "It's time for more adventure. By the way, how do you like my new outfit? I've had a fashion crisis."

It was certainly true that Aunt Tabitha didn't look like he remembered her.

On their last adventure she had been dressed from head to toe in strange flowing black wrap-around garments. Now it was skin-tight stretchy Lycra in brilliant Day-Glo hoops of colour. She still had the same enormous earrings the size of dinner plates and her fingers were still encrusted with rings, but the Lycra was new.

"Must have been quite a crisis," said Timothy, sensing with mounting excitement that he was not, after all, going to a stuffy conference full of boring people who have never even thought of crawling around in ventilation ducts. He pulled up the other window.

"Timothy Star-Mapper, World-Class Astronomer and Master of Forgotten Languages," laughed Uncle Peregrine, taking a swig of Jungle Juice from a gourd and then thrusting it at Timothy to try. He wore a brightly-coloured jacket made of many different patches all sewn together higgledy-piggledy. Hanging from it or sticking out of the pockets were interesting items such as spanners, spoons, bones, skulls of small beasts, dark blue bottles and leather pouches. He pointed to the gourd.

"New recipe. Best Jungle Juice yet. Mellow, fruity, but with a fizzy refreshing tang," he said.

Timothy took a gulp.

"Wow, this is vintage stuff," he sang at the top of his voice, bouncing up and down on his bed. "I hope there's plenty more."

Aunt Tabitha reached into her hamper, pulled out a fresh bacon sandwich and was about to offer it to Timothy when the door burst open. Peregrine and Tabitha ducked out of sight and Timothy, who was standing on his bed waving the gourd about, turned to see his parents in their dressing-gowns looking cross and bleary-eyed.

"What's that?" said his father, pointing at the gourd.

"I can smell bacon," said his mother. "And why's the window open?"

Mr and Mrs Thompson went over to the window and stuck their heads out. Uncle Peregrine and Aunt Tabitha were crouched on top of their home-made Y-shaped ladder-for-two, finishing their bacon sandwiches.

"Good morning," they said rather too politely.

"Sandwich?"

"Juice?"

Chapter 3

No one, no matter how sensible, can resist hot bacon sandwiches, so Aunt Tabitha and Uncle Peregrine were allowed to climb in and everybody munched a picnic breakfast on the bed.

"They've come to look after me while you go to the emergency conference," said Timothy between mouthfuls.

"That's all very well," said his father, "but the arrangements have been made now, so you'll have to come and be content to play with the other scientists' children."

Timothy clutched his sides and made groaning noises as if he was going to be sick.

"Oh great, the riveting company of spooky kids with enormous foreheads and names like Dominic and Quark who talk in sing-songy voices about how important their mummies and daddies are."

"That may be so…" began his father.

"But Uncle Peregrine and Aunt Tabitha can't be trusted to keep you out of trouble," finished his mother, who was more direct.

"We prefer to think of it as having adventures," said Uncle Peregrine, who tried to smile in reassuring way and look innocent, but the luminous dangle-dolly skeleton on his lapel rather spoilt the effect.

"Timothy will get into trouble wherever he goes," continued Aunt Tabitha rather more expertly. "He might as well be with us so that he doesn't embarrass you again in front of the Secretary General."

There was a pause while the Thompsons digested this fact and realized they'd been hopelessly out-manoeuvred.

"Okay," said his father grudgingly. "But make sure you get to school today even though it is the weekend tomorrow."

And with that it was settled.

A bit later, the taxi arrived to take Timothy's parents to the airport. Once they'd been waved off it was time for school.

Timothy put the Violetta Stone on the dashboard of the van with his lunch box and map-barrel.

Aunt Tabitha drove and Timothy sat on the seat next to her, doing the gears.

"What's this?" enquired Uncle Peregrine, picking up the Violetta Stone and turning it over in his hands. "Looks like ancient Hieroglyphs, but not Egyptian."

"That's right. They're Mesopotamian," replied Timothy, turning the stone up the right way. "It's from the school museum. I've been translating it."

Aunt Tabitha deftly swung the van in through the school gates and past the headmaster, who was so surprised that he cycled into the school duck pond and fell over. Next she turned into the playground and parked the van exactly in the middle, right over the hopscotch patch.

"Hasn't it been translated already?" she asked, turning off the engine.

"It was, ages ago, but it was the headmaster's ancestor, Sir Stanley Boggins, who did it and he got it completely wrong."

The headmaster came striding purposefully towards them, squirting water from his shoes and brandishing his bicycle pump. Timothy grabbed his equipment and jumped down from the cab.

"I'll tell you all about it later," he called back quietly. "Better still, try to sneak in to assembly this morning, I'm giving a talk." With that he ran off, pursued by the headmaster who was shouting something about Goths, Visigoths, Huns and Vandals.

Inside, the whole school had gathered to hear Timothy's talk. He pinned his star charts and a large drawing of the Violetta Stone to a board and then struck up his lecturer's pose: one foot in front, one behind, one hand on his hip and the other gripping the end of his copper map-barrel to use as a pointer.

"As everyone knows," he began with a tap of the drawing, "the Violetta Stone was discovered over a hundred years ago by a former pupil of the school who also decoded the hieroglyphics."

At this point the headmaster, whose great-great-grandfather had decoded it, preened himself by smoothing down the greasy flap of hair on the back of his neck, which was just as well because it meant that he didn't see Aunt Tabitha and Uncle Peregrine pop their heads over the window-sill.

"Sir Stanley Boggins declared that the coded message was nothing more than an ancient and not very good recipe for cheese toasties," he continued. Everyone groaned because, it being Friday, they knew they would have to eat the disgusting pongy mush made from the ancient recipe for lunch and that Boggins the headmaster would stand over them until they finished it. It was a tradition going back to when the stone was discovered.

"In fact it is not a recipe at all but a description of the Ancient Mesopotamians' flight to the moon."

Boggins sat up with a jolt.

"Oh yes, and what makes you think you know better than generations of famous archaeologists," he sneered, looking forward to the end of assembly so that he could give Timothy loads of punishments for insulting his family.

"Because last night I cracked the code properly," announced Timothy proudly.

An expectant hush fell on the room.

The other teachers all leaned forward with interest.

This kid was good.

"What the stone actually says is that thousands of years ago, when the Mesopotamian Empire covered half the known world, a giant comet threatened the earth. Hour by hour it grew until it looked as though it would surely smash into the earth and destroy it." Timothy picked up the stone and walked slowly up and down in front of everyone as he continued.

"Then the moon suddenly moved from its normal position in the sky and came so close to the earth that it was possible to look down into individual craters. By doing so, the moon placed itself in the path of the comet and saved the world. After that the moon went back into its normal orbit but two strange-coloured beings were accidentally left behind in a Mesopotamian seaside village. They were called moon-bugs and it's this race of beings that steered the moon about the sky."

Timothy paused for effect. The juniors sat open-mouthed in the front row, the teachers looked at their hymn books and the headmaster ground his teeth.

There was silence for a second or two and then Steven Purkiss the school bully started sniggering. Soon the whole hall was laughing at Timothy and the headmaster didn't even try to stop them.

Timothy felt himself going red.

"It's true," he shouted above the din. "The moon-bugs showed the Mesopotamians how to fly their boats in space so they could take them back home through dangerous asteroids and everything."

The laughing got even louder.

"Anyway, you'd better hope it's true because last night I spotted a comet coming straight towards the earth out of Orion's tummy and unless the moon-bugs get cracking and move the moon right now we'll all be atomized."

Hysterical laughter.

"So don't make any plans for the weekend."

By now Boggins the headmaster was getting very red in the face and dribbling with rage because he thought Timothy was making fun of his ancestor. At the same time the older kids kept the action going by making as much noise as they could. Timothy looked over to the window. Aunt Tabitha was giving Steven Purkiss one of her especial looks and Uncle Peregrine was pointing at the school television and making turn-it-on signs with his hand. Timothy rushed over to the screen and pushed a button marked "Only to be operated under the supervision of a responsible adult blah blah". The television came on with a pop.

"Here is a news flash," said the announcer in a very serious voice. Timothy turned up the volume.

"Astronomers and scientists have just announced that a strange light appeared in the middle of Orion last night. It is, as many feared, a very large and fast-moving comet and it is heading straight for planet earth."

Everyone went pale and quiet, except Steven Purkiss who was crying because of Aunt Tabitha's look.

"Schoolboy astronomer Timothy Thompson discovered the comet in the early hours of the morning whilst he was mapping the belt of Orion for a project," the announcer continued, as a picture of Timothy with his telescope and copper map-barrel flashed up on the screen.

Observing this, everyone looked round with new respect and admiration for Timothy, but he was nowhere to be seen.

"He's running across the playground with a couple of weirdos," pointed out Steven Purkiss between sobs, keen to get his own back on Aunt Tabitha. "They're going to that smelly old removal van with a crane on top."

The three friends made a strange sight as they ran along. Aunt Tabitha with her earrings jangling and a picnic hamper held above her head, Uncle Peregrine's marsupial skeletons rattling together, and Timothy with the Violetta Stone balanced in one hand and his map-barrel in the other.

"What's the plan, Timothy scientist?" wheezed Aunt Tabitha, catching her breath and climbing into the cab after him. She fished a box with four frosty blue bulbs and one black bulb on the top out of the glove compartment.

"I want to go to the moon. I think there might be something wrong because it hasn't started to do anything odd yet, like move out of orbit and get in the way of the comet."

Aunt Tabitha turned the device on as Uncle Peregrine climbed up behind the wheel on the other side. The first blue light winked on.

"It's a Kometometer," she explained. "Had it rattling around in here for years. Never knew when it might be handy. The nearer the comet gets to impact the more blue lights come on."

"What about the black light?" asked Timothy pointing.

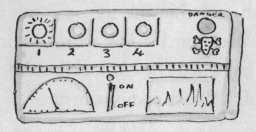

"When that comes on you try to be somewhere else," she replied with a shiver and a rattle of her earrings. "It's called the Doomsday Lamp."

"I think this might be the chance we've been looking for to test our new and highly experimental removal van modifications," said Uncle Peregrine, flipping the safety cap off a large yellow knob in the dashboard. "Buckle up everyone," he ordered, and pushed the knob down decisively with the ball of his thumb.

Chapter 4

From deep inside the van there began the throaty rumble and high-pitched whirring which Timothy, with the broad grin of adventure, instantly recognized as high compression hydraulics.

As he snapped his seat-belt shut, one whole panel of the dashboard in front of him slid away to reveal a control console covered in interesting-looking buttons, busy little dials and eager flashing lights. In the middle was a joystick and two round knobs on the ends of highly-polished brass levers. One was red and the other was green.

"The red one is for the port and the green one for the starboard engines," explained Uncle Peregrine.

By now all the children and teachers – led by Mr Boggins and Steven Purkiss – were streaming out of the school and running towards the van. Boggins reached it first and banged on Aunt Tabitha's window, whilst shouting and going a funny colour.

"I wonder what he wants," she said, and wound down her window a little to hear, but not so far that he could stick his purple head in.

"May I help in some way?" she enquired mildly.

"Give me back my stone and get this wreck out of my playground," he bellowed needlessly.

Aunt Tabitha looked at Timothy, who shook his head.

"No can do on the stone front I'm afraid, old boy," she said irritatingly. "But better news with the van thingy. Stand clear."

With that she shut the window, flipped up the safety cover on a big blue button and whacked it down with the palm of her hand. Immediately, the noise of the hydraulics increased and the van began to tilt up on its end so that the cab pointed to the sky. The three astronauts lay on their backs looking at the clouds whilst the Violetta Stone and map-barrel rolled off the dashboard and had to be found new homes.

All around the onlookers fled to the edge of the playground and cars going by slowed down to watch. From the sides of the van two round engines, which looked like pumpkins but much bigger, emerged and locked into place. Each one had a bright chrome nozzle which pointed at the ground and smoked gently. One by one all the dials moved up to show "full", "max" or "ready to go" and every light that felt like coming on did.

"Take off please, Timothy," ordered Captain Peregrine.

"Take off, aye," replied Timothy, grabbing the red and green knobs and pushing them slowly forward as far as they would go.

At once there was a tremendous whooshing noise from the engines and powdery green smoke engulfed the van as it lifted off and melted the hopscotch patch.

"Jungle Juice for fuel," explained Aunt Tabitha, knuckling half a dozen switches so that the radar screen lit up. It was blank except for a single blip.

She peered closely at the blip.

"Jumbo Jet," she called above the din, but Timothy couldn't really see the screen because his head had suddenly got so heavy he couldn't lift it.

"G force," he said to himself and felt his whole body pressed back into the seat as the rocket van hurtled towards the clouds, the green smoke streaming out behind them.

"Hold tight," called Uncle Peregrine as they entered the cotton-wool mass and the van started to shudder with the lumpiness of the wet air. Then, just as suddenly as it had entered the clouds, the van emerged out of the top into brilliant sunshine and a bright blue sky.

Five miles up, the pilot of the Jumbo Jet saw the outline of a van rush past him, its wheels turning in the breeze and two streams of what looked like green powder in the air behind it. He didn't tell anyone – instead he put the plane on autopilot, got out an inflatable cushion and had a nice lie-down in the back of the cockpit.

Higher and higher the van hurtled, leaving a sweet-smelling, green trail in its wake.

As they all looked ahead into the rich blueness, a strange thing began to happen.

"The sky's getting darker," called Timothy happily. "Just like the Mesopotamians said it would." And sure enough, the sky turned a darker and darker blue until, even though the sun was shining, they cleared the earth's atmosphere, it went black, and the stars came out.

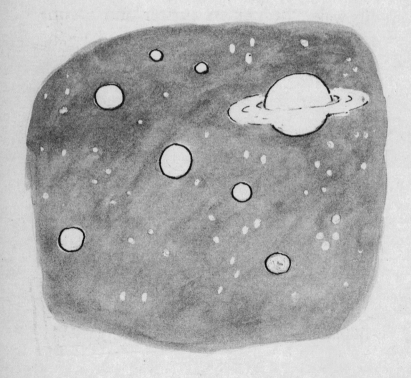

Timothy felt a lump in his throat, for this was something that he had wanted to see all his life. Gone were the street lights and towns and pollution of earth that spoilt the view. All around him more stars than he had ever seen before shone steady and strong. There were galaxies spinning and sparking like giant fire-wheels, the planets Jupiter and Saturn glowing as if they were creamy light bulbs, and the Milky Way, a glittering brush-stroke of tiny stars, painted across half the sky. All of them were as clear and bright as if they had just been made.

At that moment there was a little pop from the dashboard.

"Second light on the Kometometer," announced Aunt Tabitha. "Three more to doomsday."

Timothy looked behind them out of the side window at the beautiful green, white and blue ball of the earth and sighed, for there rushing ever nearer was the angry shimmering comet, now as big as a pomegranate. Suddenly he felt very proud of his home planet.

"Don't worry little earth," he whispered, "we'll save you."

Uncle Peregrine adjusted the red and green throttles and pushed the joystick this way and that until the van was aimed straight at the moon. Then he turned off the seat-belt sign and turned on the "Please Snack" sign.

Aunt Tabitha opened a tin of sandwiches.

"Bloater paste?" she said, handing them round. Everyone had got quite hungry with the excitement of take-off and gratefully munched their sandwiches in silence, looking at the amazing view.

Afterwards they washed their snack down with a good drink of Jungle Juice from the extra large expedition gourd.

Suddenly the radar started bleeping.

"Thousands of rocks ahead," announced Aunt Tabitha, peering into the radar screen and adjusting a few knobs to show that she was in control of the situation.

Uncle Peregrine pushed his face to the windscreen and looked about.

"Where are we, Timothy navigator?" he asked.

Timothy pulled the Violetta Stone on to his lap and ran his fingers across the carving as he translated.

" '*When the sea of stones appears*
Take great care he who steers
For all around you danger lies
In the rocky shipwreck skies,' "

he read out loud.

"I wonder what it means," pondered Aunt Tabitha absent-mindedly, as she gently pulled the last pickled onion up from the depths of a big value jar with her tongs and popped it into her mouth.

Just then, a rock that looked like a gnarled potato (except that it was as big as a house) whizzed across the nose of the van, taking a wing mirror with it.

"Giant space spuds, eh?" she exclaimed, hastily putting the lid on to the pickles jar and shoving the picnic hamper under her seat. "More like galactic mash if I've any say in the matter," she added, with a menacing rattle of her earrings.

"It's an asteroid belt," said Timothy. "And we are going too fast."

"Positions, everyone," called Uncle Peregrine as if it was the most normal thing in the universe for them to be millions of miles from home in a tatty removal van, dodging intergalactic potatoes.

"Bandit one o'clock high," called Aunt Tabitha from the radar, imitating a fighter pilot and donning her battle goggles.

Timothy looked up and a bit right at

the one o'clock position. At first there was nothing and then a speck appeared and grew faster than anything he'd ever seen before. The asteroid was tumbling towards them at an incredible speed.

Timothy promptly pulled back on the throttles to engage retro-thrust. The van shuddered and slowed. Uncle Peregrine threw the joystick over and sent the van diving to one side. As it did so the wheels brushed the underside of the potato-shaped rock, which by now had become the size of a speeding supertanker.

"Hostiles nine and twelve o'clock," called Aunt Tabitha, warming to her task.

"Check," called back Timothy, seeing them both coming and speeding up in the hope that Uncle Peregrine would be able to steer between them.

At that moment a bossy trilling sound filled the cab.

Uncle Peregrine tapped one of the dials.

"Nearly out of fuel – situation critical,"

he announced, pulling a cork from the top of the dashboard and shoving a funnel in.

Timothy grabbed the joystick and just managed to zoom between the two asteroids as Uncle Peregrine tipped Jungle Juice down the funnel and into the engines.

On and on they hurtled through the inky blackness of space, dodging this way and that to avoid the tumbling asteroids. As each one approached Aunt Tabitha called from the radar screen whilst Timothy and Uncle Peregrine expertly shoved the controls back and forth, each one anticipating the other's moves until they were working as a perfect team.

Chapter 5

Hundreds of gnarled potato-shaped rocks later, and with only a few dents and gouges to the body of the van, they shot out of the asteroid belt and back into empty space.

In the cab the Kometometer popped and the third bulb came on.

"The comet has grown so much that Orion's hardly visible," observed Uncle Peregrine, as they turned back on course for the moon which was now much nearer.

Timothy felt queasy.

"Something's definitely not right," he said, following his finger along the code on the stone and translating to himself. "The moon-bugs definitely promised the Mesopotamians that they'd go on protecting the earth. After all, they've done it for millions of years, that's why the face of the moon has so many craters in it: all the comets and meteorites crashed there."

"What about the comet that killed the dinosaurs?" enquired Aunt Tabitha.

Timothy spun the Violetta Stone round a bit and checked his translation.

"They let that one through because the dinosaurs were getting too big for their boots and trampling over all the smaller furry animals."

"The moon's exactly where it normally is," put in Uncle Peregrine, peering ahead and squinting. "And it shows no signs of moving from its orbit. Perhaps everyone's going to be atomized after all," he continued. "At least there'll be no more school or traffic wardens. That's one consolation." This cheered them up for a bit, until they realized that it also meant no more trees, no more bloater paste and no more friends.

"Maybe it's because we've been so unkind to other animals – like the dinosaurs were," said Timothy gloomily.

Just when everything looked at its blackest, and the fate of the world hung in the balance, two good things came along almost at once as they often do in a crisis.

"Disgustingly rich chocolate cake with extra thick fudge icing?" asked Aunt Tabitha, pulling a round tin out of the picnic hamper.

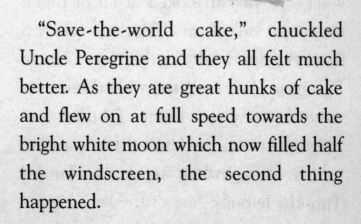

"Save-the-world cake," chuckled Uncle Peregrine and they all felt much better. As they ate great hunks of cake and flew on at full speed towards the bright white moon which now filled half the windscreen, the second thing happened.

There was a splutt on the glass and a rubbery-looking creature about the size of a set of bagpipes lay pressed against it, looking in. The alien had three legs, each ending in a round sucker, three arms with little fingers and three eyes on stumpy stalks. At first it looked at all of them: one eye on Aunt Tabitha, one on Timothy and the other on Uncle Peregrine, but very soon all three eyes were looking at Aunt Tabitha and bulging even more than to start with.

"It's a moon-bug scout," exclaimed Timothy happily.

"And it looks just like me," said Aunt Tabitha. "It must be very intelligent and come from a highly advanced civilization to have such up-to-the-minute dress sense."

As he looked, Timothy saw that the moon-bug's skin was just like stretchy Lycra and coloured in bright Day-Glo hoops the same as Aunt Tabitha.

Uncle Peregrine attracted the moon-bug's attention with his dangle-dolly and pointed at the comet which was now bigger than ever. The moon-bug looked at the comet, pointed at it with one hand, at the earth with the other and then at the moon with all three.

"I think he wants us to go and help," decided Timothy, as the moon-bug moved on its suckers to the front of the bonnet and pointed to where it wanted them to go.

Down and down they went towards the moon and, under the moon-bug's direction, settled in to a very low orbit.

"He's taking us to the dark side," whispered Timothy, gratefully accepting another bloater paste sandwich from Aunt Tabitha. As he spoke, the shadow of the van stretched out further and further in front of them until the sun dipped below the horizon behind them and they flew on, only dimly able to see the moonscape below.

"Sunset on the moon," breathed Timothy with pleasure as he made a diagram in his notebook.

One by one, they were joined by other stripy Day-Glo moon-bugs who zoomed along the surface next to the van. They weaved about, ducking and diving like dolphins round a ship.

"I think their stripes help them fly," theorized Timothy as he drew a moon-bug in his notebook. And he was right, for as the others watched they saw the moon-bugs' coloured stripes pulsating as they flew along.

Suddenly the van shot over the rim of the crater and the ground fell away for hundreds of metres. In the middle of the crater was the most amazing sight. In the eerie glow from the stars and comet, something towered up at an odd angle into the sky.

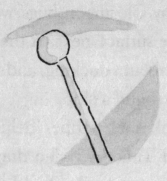

Chapter 6

"Yoicks," said Aunt Tabitha.

"Spotlight on," announced Uncle Peregrine, flicking a switch and sending a spreading beam of light washing over the strange object.

"It's a shiny metal tower, but there's no windows in it or anything," observed Timothy. "And it's leaning over to one side."

Aunt Tabitha consulted the radar. "It's bigger than the leaning tower of Pisa but smaller than the Eiffel tower," she said.

Uncle Peregrine trained the light on the top. "And there's a huge stripy Day-Glo ball on the end."

They all wondered what the purpose of this strange structure was.

"Perhaps it's ancient Modern Art," suggested Aunt Tabitha, but as they manoeuvred closer they saw that all the moon-bugs had collected on the stripy ball and glued themselves on with their suckers.

"I've counted a hundred and fifty-seven bugs in all," said Aunt Tabitha.

"The ones at the back are pushing and the ones on the front are pulling," replied Timothy, thinking that it all reminded him of something very familiar and then, with a rush, he realized what it was.

"It's a giant switch for controlling the moon, just like the ones in the van. The moon-bugs are trying to shift it and they can't."

"I wonder why not," mused Aunt Tabitha. "Perhaps they need vitamin supplements," she added, calculating into how many pieces she'd have to cut the save-the-world cake so that every moon-bug got a mouthful.

Just then the guide bug detached itself from the lever and landed with a splat on the roof. It took hold of the spotlight and shone it at the base of the mighty switch. The astronauts followed its beam.

"Space junk," exclaimed Uncle Peregrine and Aunt Tabitha together.

"And no ordinary space junk, either," added Timothy, shoving the joystick forward and working the levers to get a better look. "That's the International Space Station. The one with a kitchen and bunk-beds and an astrodome. The one I told them not to jettison. The one they didn't know what colour to paint."

As they looked, they saw all sorts of other junk jammed against the switch. There were bits of satellites, burnt-out rockets, several huge canisters of radioactive waste and the dragon figurehead of a Mesopotamian space-ship. But mostly there was the International Space Station which had hooked itself over the switch as if it were a hoop at a hoop-la stall.

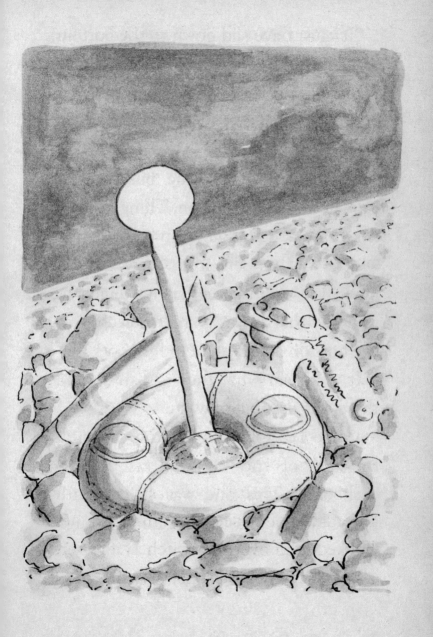

"It must have slid down to the bottom and jammed the switch solid," said Uncle Peregrine as Timothy zoomed the van around so that they could see it from all angles.

The fourth frosty blue bulb in the Kometometer plunked on. Things looked desperate and the glow from the comet which was hidden from view by the moon was so intense that it seemed to Timothy that it was going to reach over the horizon and fry him in his boots.

It was clear what they had to do and there was no time to waste.

Uncle Peregrine flipped the cover off the last of the big buttons on the dashboard. This one was striped with Day-Glo hoops just like the moon-bugs' bodies.

Aunt Tabitha eyed it with satisfaction.

"Good choice," she said as Uncle Peregrine pushed it firmly down. In the back of the van the high compression hydraulics whirred into life and the massive grab on the top shuddered into life. Timothy slipped his hand into a special glove attached to the dashboard. He lifted his gloved hand and pushed it forward. Outside, the grab shot out over the front of the van on its long arm and wiggled its fingers in time with Timothy.

"Start there," instructed Aunt Tabitha, and pointed to a burnt-out probe.

Uncle Peregrine gave the controls a few practised tweaks and the van moved crisply up to a piece of jagged space probe. Timothy worked the glove and the grab grabbed it.

"Full reverse, Uncle."

"Aye aye, Grab Master." And with that the motors whirred and the broken remains were lifted clear of the switch. For several hours they worked, pushing and pulling the junk away from the switch with the grab and cutting it into handy lengths with the giant scissor attachment. In threes and fours, the moon-bugs dragged the bits away from the switch.

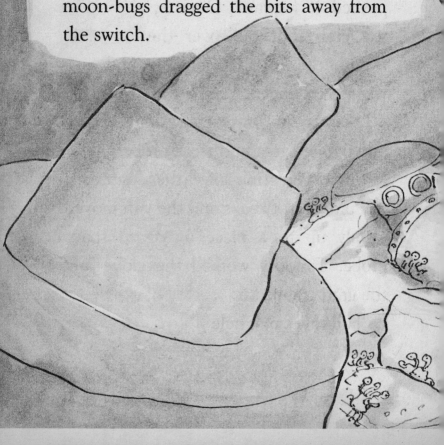

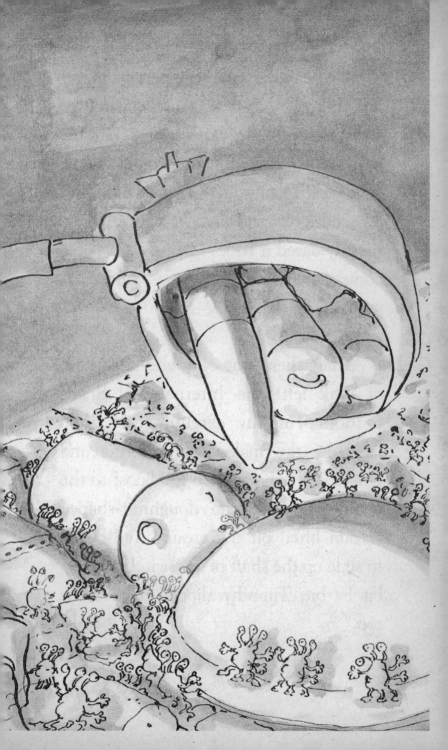

All the while the comet got bigger and bigger and nearer and nearer to smashing into the earth. Aunt Tabitha, who was looking after the Kometometer, gave the Doomsday Light one of her especial looks and silently dared it to come on. For the moment it did as it was told.

At last there was only one large item of junk left: the International Space Station. Timothy carefully took hold of it by the maker's lifting ring and Uncle Peregrine applied full boost to the engines. Slowly, the doughnut-shaped station lifted off the ground and began to slide up the shaft of the switch. Gently, bit by bit, Timothy slipped it over the top.

"It looks completely undamaged," announced Timothy, happily folding the grab up and pinning the station snugly to the top of the van.

Aunt Tabitha guessed he had plans for the station and handed him a "well done" slice of save-the-world cake. She pushed the rest through the airlock for the moon-bugs, who each took a tiny handful.

Next, the moon-bugs returned to their positions on the switch and Uncle Peregrine landed the van with a gentle whumph of moon dust.

Chapter 7

As the astronauts watched, the moon-bugs all strained again at the mighty switch and slowly, bit by bit, it began to move. Then, with a little jolt, the moon started to rumble from deep inside, sending vibrations through the wheels of the space van and into the cab.

"Here we go. Stand by for more

adventure," cried Aunt Tabitha, holding her stomach as the moon lurched violently sideways and left its normal orbit very fast indeed.

Steadily, the moon rushed to the rescue of the frightened earth and all the people who lived on it. Some of them were running around screaming, others were hiding and a few, including Timothy's mother and father, were sitting in the United Nations conference room watching with wonder as the moon rushed towards the earth on a giant television screen.

In the cockpit of the cab the astronauts were very quiet, each one watching the Kometometer and trying to work out if the moon-bugs would be in time to save the world.

"Time to become seriously famous,

Timbo my lad," said Aunt Tabitha, fiddling with a camcorder and a transmitting device. She pointed the lens at him, focused it expertly and pressed the transmit button.

"This is Timothy Thompson calling planet earth from Moon Control," he said several times and then Aunt Tabitha released the button.

"This is earth," came back a crisp voice through the loudspeaker. "Please hold, patching you through to the United Nations Emergency Council." Inside the United Nations building the Secretary General quietened down all the excited scientists who couldn't believe what they were seeing.

"Ladies unt Gentlemen," he began, "it vould appear zat even as vee speak someone called Timothy Thompson is on ze moon and in charge of Earth Rescue." Privately he vondered to himself vhy ze name seemed familiar.

The screen flickered and the loudspeaker crackled:

"Moon Control to United Nations, Earth Rescue in progress, moon to comet intercept position in one minute and counting," announced Timothy crisply into the camcorder, glancing at the read-out on the radar. The TV crews shoved their cameras forward and relayed his broadcast to the world. In their little booths the translators translated.

"But how has ziz been possible?" asked the Secretary General, who thought he recognized Timothy's voice from somewhere.

"The moon has ancient engines in it and a switch on the back which the inhabitants known as moon-bugs use to steer it into the path of comets and big meteors. It hasn't happened since the Mesopotamians' time. That's why no one knew about it."

In the hall Timothy's parents shook their heads with disbelief and the world held its breath.

"Vot is your plan?"

"We've got to get the moon between the comet and the earth so that the comet hits the light side away from us. But we might be too late."

"Vot vas the hold-up?"

"That little space station you threw away and wouldn't let me have was jamming the switch, along with a load of other junk."

The Secretary General at last recognized Timothy's voice.

"Hey, aren't you ze kid vot knocked me on ze head wiz a ventilation grille unt zen told me I'd regret it if I jettisoned ze International Space Station?" he asked, going red and rubbing a big scar above his left ear.

Fortunately, Timothy had no time to reply because at that moment the moon stopped dead in space with a terrific jolt. It was exactly in the path of the comet which by now was so close it was filling the sky. On earth everyone looked up but all they could see was the round black shadow of the moon with the eerie glow of the comet showing round its edges.

With a faintly operatic pop the fifth bulb on the 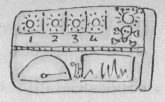 Kometometer, the black Doomsday Lamp, came on and glowed smugly.

"Hang on, me hearties," called Aunt Tabitha, as she clung tight to the door handle with one hand and waved her tongs about with the other. Outside, the moon-bugs clung to the van with their suckers. Valiant guardians of the switch though they were, they were also soft and rubbery and easily bruised. Timothy put his hand in the glove and held everyone tight to a massive moon rock with the grab.

At that moment, the comet, which had travelled billions of miles over millions of years, suddenly ended its journey on the face of the moon.

At first there was a massive flaring brightness as the comet smashed into the ground and made a huge new crater. It exploded into a million fiery fragments which shot out bright and fierce, but also small and harmless in all directions.

"Moon quake next," predicted Timothy, gripping the rock as hard as he could.

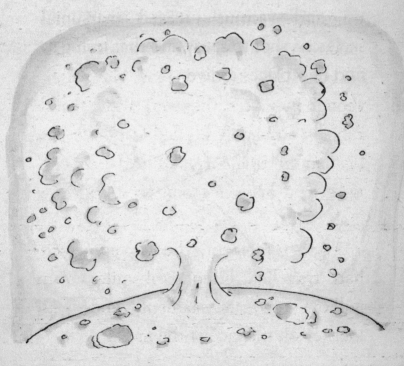

Almost immediately the ground started to bounce beneath them and the van, with the astronauts inside and the moon-bugs outside, was shaken around as if by a giant hand. Dust rose from the surface and small rocks bounced about. Inside the cab, loose items such as the Violetta Stone, the copper map-barrel, the cake tin and various unfixed marsupial skeletons shot this way and that trying to find new places to live.

Just when it seemed the van could take no more, the shock wave passed as suddenly as it had come and the moon lay still. Everyone felt themselves for broken bones and looked around to see if there was any damage. Outside, the moon-bugs all hovered about, feeling their little rubbery bodies for bruised bits.

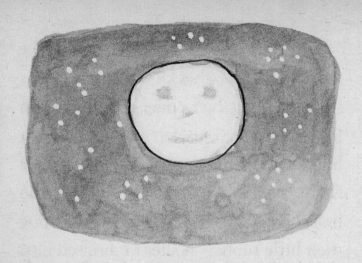

On earth, people looking up could see that the face on the moon which before only had two eyes and a mouth now had a big grey nose and looked much happier.

"The switch is okay," observed Uncle Peregrine, watching the moon-bugs as they clustered round it.

"They are about to change the setting which means it's time for us to leave," responded Timothy, flicking back the safety lid of the green button and pressing it down with a satisfying clunk.

As the engines powered up, Aunt Tabitha and one of the smaller moon-bugs exchanged gifts through the airlock. She gave it a hastily scribbled recipe for save-the-world cake whilst the moon-bug gave her a little jar of stripy Day-Glo paint.

"We should have some fun with this," she said to the others, holding the jar up to the light. "Paint it on and you become a proper moon-bug."

Noticing that the van was about to leave, the moon-bugs turned from their work. Some of them were on the switch and the others were planting the strips of junk in a ring round its base to make a fence. The sunlight shimmered and sparked off the paint and cut edges.

"It's to keep the junk off," observed Timothy approvingly as the moon-bugs did a little "goodbye" jig and waved their suckers at them.

Next, the van, carrying the little space station on its back, lifted off and dived to earth. Behind them the brave and gentle moon carried the moon-bugs back to their proper place in the inky blackness of space.

"Stand by to deploy space station," instructed Uncle Peregrine, delicately placing the van into low orbit around the earth.

"Aye aye, Captain," smiled Timothy as he lifted the glistening metal doughnut off the roof with the grab and set it gently rotating in an orbit that would take it round the world and over his home every few hours. He looked forward to using his new status as World Hero to force Boggins into letting him off school to visit it.

Perhaps Aunt Tabitha will let me paint it with her stripy paint, he thought to himself.

Beside him, the loud speaker crackled into life.

"Vell done, Timothy, you and your friends have saved ze vorld," chortled the

Secretary General, prepared, under the circumstances, to forget all about the ventilation duct incident.

In the background they could hear cheering.

"You may all ask for any revord you like."

There was a pause while they all thought about this for a bit.

"A new picnic hamper please," said Aunt Tabitha, rubbing her jewel-encrusted hands with anticipation. "This one just isn't big enough for long-range expeditions," she added, mindful that on any expedition one should always make sure one has emergency supplies for at least a week.

"A new wing mirror for the van, please," put in Uncle Peregrine, who already had everything he really wanted.

Timothy, who didn't, went for something more ambitious:

"I would like all the lights in the world turned out each Friday night for a couple of hours so that everyone can see the stars again," he said into the camcorder.

All the diplomats and scientists from around the world thought that this was a brilliant idea and congratulated the Thompsons on having such a genius for a son. Then, because it was Friday evening and everyone had heard Timothy's request, the lights started going out all over the world. People came out of their huts and houses and tents where they'd been watching the television under the kitchen table or a pile of rugs or in the cellar and gazed at a beautiful sight none of them had ever seen before: a black sky filled with millions and millions of stars that were so bright and near-looking it made them feel as if they could pick them like apples off a tree.

At the same time, miles above them, the van was entering the atmosphere and continuing to plummet earthwards.

"The bonnet is starting to glow red hot," observed Timothy, looking out over the front.

Uncle Peregrine took hold of a wooden toggle that hung from the roof of the cab on a yellow lanyard.

"Stand by to deploy drove-chutes," he said and pulled hard on the lanyard. From the back of the van three parachutes exploded and filled. With a judder the van slowed down to ordinary falling speed and dropped on towards the ground.

Aunt Tabitha turned off the radar and lay back in her seat watching the sky turn from black to blue again.

"I wonder where we are going to land," she mused happily.

In the United Nations building, as the applause and cheering slowly died away

and everyone sat down, there was a tremendous crash and part of the ceiling fell in, followed by the front of a very dented and smoking removal van. From inside Timothy waved to his parents who covered their eyes with their hands and shook their heads.

As Uncle Peregrine shut down the van's flight systems, Aunt Tabitha turned a chrome handle and kicked open the passenger door. It swung momentarily on one hinge and then crashed to the ground, narrowly missing the Secretary General.

Complete silence descended on the hall. The interpreters sat poised to translate to the world, and the television cameras whirred expectantly.

Aunt Tabitha opened her picnic hamper and held out a crisp white triangle.

"Bloater paste sandwich, anyone?" she asked cheerily.

The End